I'M NO BULLY, AM I?

Felisha Williams

Illustrations by Donnie Obina

I'm a bossy girl from around the corner of a large neighborhood. I'm known as Ke'niya McDaniel, but I like to be called Keke. I don't have many friends, but I don't care. In fact, who needs friends? They get on my nerves anyway. I like being the boss and doing things my way. Yeah, maybe I have a bad attitude... maybe; but I dare someone to do something about it. Oh, by the way, I also pack quite a punch, especially when someone makes me mad.

School is just the place for me to organize my fourth-grade classmates and do whatever I want, as long as my teachers don't see me. All was super duper until one day the weirdest thing happened to me—well, actually it wasn't weird but kind of insulting—when I was called a bully by some of my classmates. I couldn't believe it! How could I be called a bully? I had always thought that bullies were big, angry boys.

I wasn't a boy, I wasn't big, and I didn't think I was angry—well, maybe a little short-tempered, but not angry. So I was no bully, was I?

Okay, so there was that time I put gum in Kierra's hair during art class and made her cry, but it was just a little, and anyway I thought I was doing her a favor by giving her a new hairstyle.

That one time I filled Timmy's lunchbox with water while he wasn't paying attention? And that made him sad and angry? Well, that was only because I believed he really wanted to eat cafeteria food in the first place.

Of course, there was the time where I gave Carlos a wedgie as he patiently waited in line, which made him yell out in pain; but I reckoned he always wore his pants too low, so I just pulled them up for him.

I also called Stewart a midget and hurt his feelings because I believed that at three feet tall he was too short to be in the fourth grade.

And so what if I called Susie a dot-to-dot face, which made her feel ugly? I believed she had too many freckles on her face.

I didn't see what the big deal was. I always said that I was sorry for what I did whenever the teacher talked to me about it, so why was I being called a bully? Wasn't I helping these kids?

Then suddenly, I shook my head at my crazy way of thinking. I realized that my classmates had a few—well, maybe quite a lot of—reasons to believe that I was a bully. I had no excuse for my behavior. I sighed at the thought of how mean and hurtful I had been to others. "Maybe I am a bully," I whispered as I walked into the girls' bathroom.

Tears formed in my eyes as I looked at my reflection in the mirror. I had to find a special way to make it up and apologize to my classmates. After school, I ran home as fast as I could because I was ashamed of myself and didn't like who I was.

I didn't know I was a bully. I just thought that I was being tough and cool. I guess I would want to wear my hair any way I like without someone putting gum in it. And OK, I would want to eat my lunch without anyone adding water to it. And I would want to be able to wait in line without someone giving me a wedgie. And sure, I would want to be respected even if I was shorter than everyone else. And yeah, if I were born with freckles on my face, I guess I wouldn't want someone to call me a dot-to-dot face.

I would want others to treat me with kindness and respect. I would want to be a normal, happy kid who could enjoy being at school without a bully pushing me around and making me afraid to be the person that I am. I knew that this was how others wanted to be treated as well; so the next day, I apologized to all my classmates and invited them all over for an ice-cream party. With my victory voice, I stated with confidence, "I'm no bully—well, not anymore!"

To order additional copies of this book, contact:
Xlibris Corporation
1-888-795-4274
www.Xlibris.com
Orders@Xlibris.com

CPSIA information can be obtained
at www.ICGtesting.com
Printed in the USA
LVHW07n1710160718
583926LV00010B/153/P